**BOOK ONE
STARABELLA
AT HOME**

Mystery Girl of Music

Written by Sharon Fialco

Based on Music Composed and Performed by Tara Fialco

Narrated and Sung by Dana Fialco

Illustrated by Anton Petrov

PLAY THE CD TO HEAR THE STORY AND MUSIC
CAPTIONS ARE INCLUDED IN THE BOOK

Fialco Productions, Inc.

OTHER BOOKS IN THE STARABELLA SERIES

STARABELLA
New Adventures and Mixed Emotions

STARABELLA
Welcome to a Bright New World

CD RECORDINGS ALSO AVAILABLE
The Three-Book Series Music Soundtrack

The CD Single "A New Beginning"

Published by Fialco Productions, Inc.
205 E. 95th Street, Suite 30K
New York, NY 10128

business@starabella.com

Copyright © and ℗ 2010 by Fialco Productions, Inc.
Art Direction by Sharon Fialco
Book Design by Susanna Yoffe, CG+M Advertising, New York, NY

All rights reserved.
No portion of this book or recording may be reproduced—mechanically, electronically, or by any other means, including, without limitation, photocopying, recording, and digital transfer—without the prior written permission of the publisher and copyright owner, Fialco Productions, Inc.
Printed in China

SUMMARY: Mr. and Mrs. Oclaif bring home their new baby girl to find she is full of mystery and surprise; her eyes shine like stars when she is happy, and though she has trouble communicating with words as she begins to grow up, she has a special talent that allows her to express her thoughts and feelings through music.

Publisher's Cataloging-in-Publication Data
(Prepared by The Donohue Group, Inc.)

Fialco, Sharon.
   Starabella / written by Sharon Fialco ; based on music composed and performed by Tara Fialco ; narrated and sung by Dana Fialco ; illustrated by Anton Petrov.

     v. : col. ill. ; cm. + sound discs. -- (Starabella : bright new world series)

   This collection was inspired by the childhood music and experiences of the author's daughter, Tara. Dealing with autism, Tara composed music to express her thoughts and feelings.
   CD recording produced by Joe Vulpis, AP Music, Inc.
   Each book contains a note at head of title: Bk.1. Starabella at home -- bk.2. Starabella in the community -- bk.3. Starabella at school.
   Each book has an accompanying CD containing the narrated story with music.
   Summary: The story of Starabella, a musically talented little girl with learning differences, full of mystery and surprise.
   Incomplete contents: Bk. 1. Mystery girl of music -- bk. 2. New adventures and mixed emotions -- bk. 3. Welcome to a bright new world
   ISBN: 978-0-9715880-3-5 (set)

1. Autistic children--Juvenile fiction. 2. Mainstreaming in education--Juvenile fiction. 3. Musical ability--Juvenile fiction. 4. Inclusive education--Juvenile fiction. 5. Social interaction in children--Juvenile fiction. 6. Learning disabilities--Juvenile fiction. 7. Autistic children--Fiction. 8. Mainstreaming in education--Fiction. 9. Musical ability--Fiction. 10. Learning disabilities--Fiction. I. Fialco, Tara. II. Fialco, Dana. III. Petrov, Anton, 1977- IV. Vulpis, Joe. V. AP Music Entertainment, Inc. VI. Title.

PZ7.F53 S73 2010
[Fic]
2009906619

Library of Congress Control Number: 2009906619
ISBN: 978-0-9715880-0-4

To order your copy of Book One, Book Two, Book Three, the complete three-book series, the three-book series music soundtrack, or the CD single "A New Beginning," please visit www.starabella.com.

Introduction

Mr. and Mrs. Oclaif are jubilant. They have just brought home their baby girl. They are astonished to see that when their little daughter smiles, her eyes shine like stars! They name her Starabella ("Starry" for short). Mysteriously, the stars in the evening sky seem to sparkle and dance in celebration of Starabella's birth. **DOES STARABELLA HAVE A SPECIAL CONNECTION TO THE STARS?**

Children who listen to and read this story might discover that Starry has some experiences and emotions similar to their own. Starry impresses her parents and grandparents with her extraordinary abilities and amazing musical talent. Sometimes, however, she exhibits unusual behavior, which confuses her parents. In turn, her parents' reaction to this behavior confuses Starry. **ABOVE ALL, MR. AND MRS. OCLAIF WISH FOR STARRY'S EYES TO CONTINUE TO SHINE AND FOR HER TO KNOW SHE IS ALWAYS THEIR LITTLE STAR.**

This story was inspired by the childhood music and experiences of the author's daughter Tara. Dealing with autism, Tara composed music to create a magical, musical world of empathy, acceptance of others, and acceptance of self.

Guide to Listening to & Reading This Story

This book contains illustrated pages and a fully narrated CD, complete with page-turn instructions. The illustrations include captions taken from the narration to help listeners follow along. The combined audio and visual presentation of the story enhances comprehension.

When children listen to this story with a caring adult, the CD can be paused at various points to provide opportunities for discussion of feelings and ideas prompted by the story.

Since the story is narrated, children also have the option to listen to the story on their own.

Children can use the illustrations as a guide to retell the story in their own words when not listening to the CD.

PLEASE ENJOY THE STORY AND SING, DANCE, DREAM, AND IMAGINE ALONG WITH THE MUSIC.

Chapter One
A Star Is Born

Dawn. A new beginning. Magically, stars can still be seen shining through the morning mist.

Something very special happened one day to Mr. and Mrs. Oclaif. Their baby girl was born.

Mommy exclaimed, "Look, Daddy! When our little girl is happy, her eyes shine like stars!"

Bliing! Bliing! Bling!

"WELCOME TO THE WORLD, STARABELLA," chimed Mommy and Daddy together.

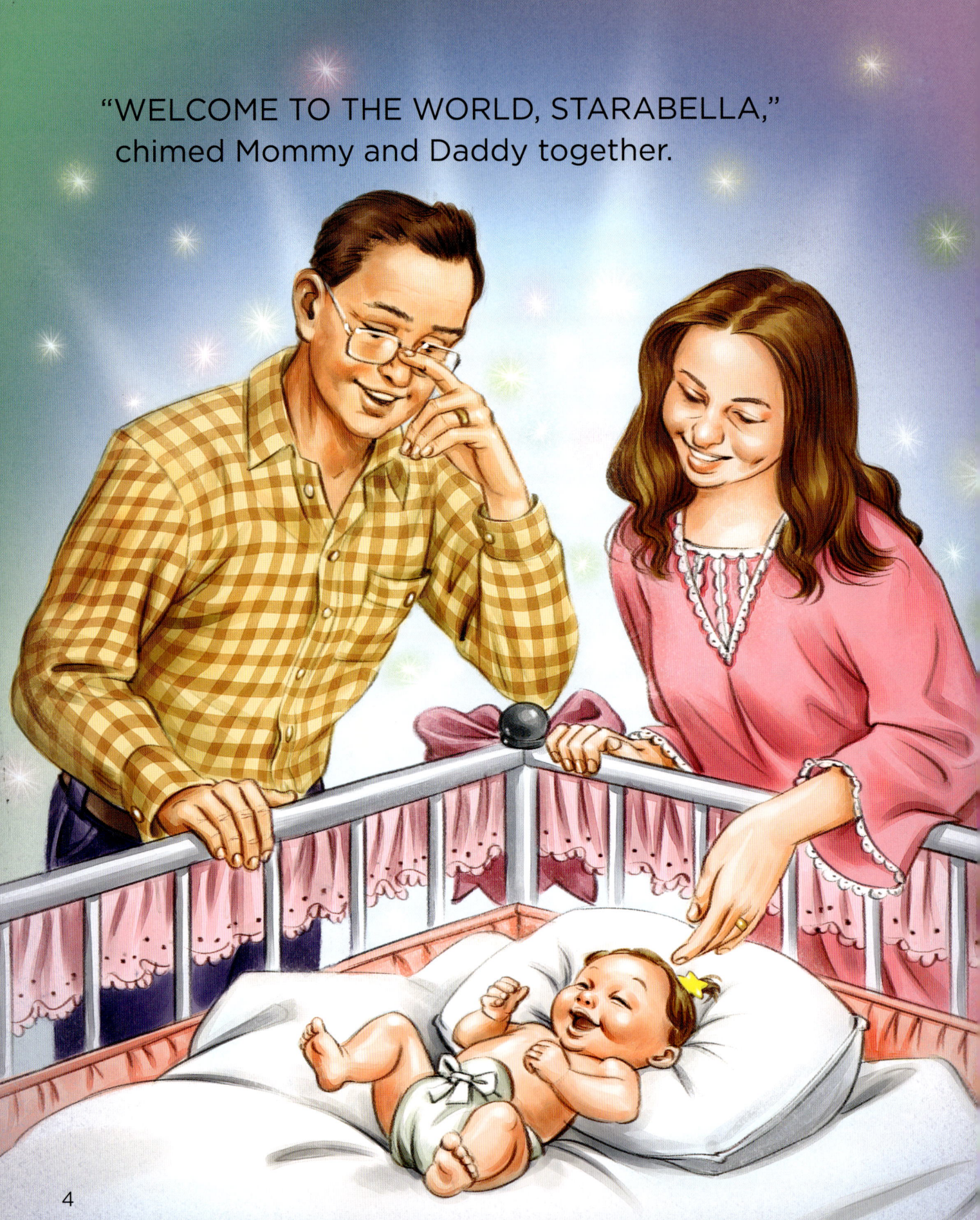

Outside, a dazzling display of glittery lights sparkled and danced in the evening sky.

As Starabella's eyelids began to close, she could hear Mommy singing a song that she made up from the love inside her.

Starabella's Lullaby

Shhh. Starabella's sleeping. What might she be dreaming about?

It's a mystery.

LYRICS: PAGE 26

Chapter Two
The Star Begins to Shine

Starabella truly did become the ★ *Star* ★ of her family as she began to grow up. She was in the spotlight of everyone's attention.

"Come to me, Starry," encouraged Mommy. "That's my girl!"

Starabella's eyes shined like stars.

While other babies were still crawling and scooting around, Starabella was running and climbing.

Starabella was always happy when her two most favorite people in the whole world came to visit. They were her grandparents and greatest admirers, Rose and Ray. Starabella called them "RoRo" and "RayRay."

Welcome to Our House

Mommy and Daddy knew their little star was fantastic. Yet, some things about her behavior began to puzzle them.

Sometimes Starabella felt like she was alone in her own world.

*Feelings of the Past
(Instrumental)*

"Don't be sad, little Starry."

"Please know that we always love you."

"You are our shining star."

It's a Mystery

Chapter Three
The Big Surprise

Ahhhhh!
What a lazy morning.
Ahhhhh!

Starry saw a cute little red ladybug with black dots crawling across the windowpane.

"Hi, little lady," said Mommy.

Starry was fascinated by the zigzag path the ladybug was taking.

She hummed a little tune to keep her tiny, polka-dotted friend company on her journey.

Lazy Ladybug Morning
(Instrumental)

Starabella noticed a great big truck pull into her driveway.

Mommy called,
"Come, Starry!
Come see the
BIG SURPRISE!"

"Shall I read the note aloud?" asked Mommy.

To Our Favorite Musical Star,

We noticed how much you enjoy playing on this piano when you come to visit us. Since no one in our home plays it any longer, we want you to have it in your home to enjoy. Perhaps you'll play it for us when we come to visit you.

Love, love, love,
Your Number One Fans,
RoRo and RayRay

P.S. Try not to bang on it.

"Thank you, thank you, ladybug!!!"

Feeling like the luckiest girl in the world, Starabella ran in circles around the piano.

Her eyes shined like stars.

Bliing! Bliing! Bliing!

To show her excitement, sorry to say—bang on her new piano, Starabella did. She hit high notes. She hit low notes. She hit notes in between.

It was driving Mommy and Daddy berserk.

Determination

LYRICS: PAGE 29

Even Kitten Kaboodle Oclaif, the family's pet cat, was excited. She liked to play along with Starabella by running across the piano keys.

Kitten Kaboodle

Starry and Kitten Kaboodle rubbed noses.
Purrrrrrr.

Starabella's eyes shined like stars.

Bliing! *Bliing!* *Bliing!*

In the Oclaif home, there was harmony.

25

Starabella Musical Numbers

STARABELLA'S LULLABY

**Lullaby, little baby
Lullaby, little love
Lullaby, my sweet angel
My gift from stars above**

**Lullaby, little baby
Lullaby, go to bed
Lullaby, go to sleep now
Sweet dreams, now rest your head**

RAP

If you are looking for fun
This is where it's at
Pull up a chair
But don't you dare
Sit on their cat

WELCOME TO OUR HOUSE

Welcome, welcome, welcome,
  welcome, welcome, welcome
Look who's here—give a cheer!
Good to see you—well,
  how are you?
Welcome, welcome to
  our house!

So glad you chose to come
  our way
We just can't wait to share
  this day
So come on in—we hope
  you'll stay to
Sit awhile, chat awhile
Oh, please, let's all
  have some food
(Sit awhile, chat awhile—
  have some food)
We'll fill our hearts and
  tummies and lift the mood

Welcome, welcome, welcome,
  welcome, welcome, welcome
Look who's here—give a cheer!
Good to see you—well,
  how are you?
Welcome, welcome to
  our house!

We have a place here
  just for you
We love to hear
  your laughter, too
We'll all tell stories
  old and new
And joke a little, smile a lot,
  and play—
And sing a song
(Joke a little, smile a lot,
  and sing a song)
We wish you could stay
  all day long!

IT'S A MYSTERY

It's a mystery, not knowing
Anything that lies ahead
And someday it may all make sense
But it's a mystery till then

It's a mystery no matter how
Life can be to figure out
And though my love will never end
It's a mystery till then

And until the day it all makes sense
It's a mystery till then

DETERMINATION

Determination—
 it's building up fast
She's determined
 and it's going to last
Determination—
 she's got that fire
Watch that girl inspire

She's got determination
With a soul of creation
She's got determination
She's a star—
Determination's gonna
 get her far

Determination—she's gonna
 keep tryin'
She's determined and soon
 she'll be flyin'
Determination—she's
 workin' it out
What's it all about?

She's got determination
With a soul of creation
She's got determination
She's a star—
Determination's gonna
 get her far

Determination—she's
 building up steam
She's determined to go after
 her dream
Determination—and she's
 got a lot
What has that girl got?

She's got determination
With a soul of creation
She's got determination
She's a star—

She's got determination
With a soul of creation
She's got determination
She's a star—
Determination's gonna
 get her far

THE SEASONS FLOW WITH MUSIC
(Narration over instrumental)

Listen.
It's spring—
The season of birth.
Do you hear the gentle rain?
Can you picture little buds poking their heads
  through the earth?
They rise up to the sun.
Feel and hear the sweetness of the soft breeze.
The music is happy.
People are happy.

The music becomes stronger
 as the sun becomes brighter.
It's summer.
The music slows down because it is hotter.
Suddenly, there's a burst of color.
Hear it?
The earth is in full bloom.
Can you see the flowers?
Nature sings as bees buzz and birds chirp.
Fireworks explode in the night sky.
People are celebrating.

Colors begin to fade.
It's cooler.
People feel a little sad.
It's autumn.
Do you hear the change in the music?
As leaves turn to red, orange,
 and gold, spirits rise.
The wind gusts.
Hear it blow?
The leaves are lifted in swirling circles
 by the wind before falling to the ground.
Can you hear and see them fall?

**Now the music is brewing up
 a howling, angry storm.
It's freezing.
Winter is here.
Snow falls boldly.
Listen—you can hear it.
Picture it filling the sky.
The music sounds brighter.
The earth is covered with a
 glistening blanket of white.
Plants are asleep.
Shhh.
Do you hear sleigh bells?
People are filled with joy.
It's holiday time!**

**Hear the quiet, gentle rain?
Spring has come around once again.
Nature awakens.**

KITTEN KABOODLE

Kitten Kaboodle,
  Kitten Kaboodle
You are so cute and soft
  and fat
Kitten Kaboodle,
  Kitten Kaboodle
Oh, how we love this cat,
  our cat
She rubs up against us
  to ask for love
And begs and pleads for food
She roams all around and
  pokes in her nose
Right where it doesn't belong
And puts us in a bad mood—
How rude!

Kitten Kaboodle,
  Kitten Kaboodle
You are a special cat,
  our cat

Kitten Kaboodle,
  Kitten Kaboodle
Oh, how we love this cat,
  our cat
She rubs up against us
  to ask for love
And begs and pleads for food
She roams all around and
  pokes in her nose
Right where it doesn't belong
And puts us in a bad mood—
How rude!

Kitten Kaboodle
  Kitten Kaboodle
You are a special cat—
Our cat

Book One Recording Credits

PERFORMANCES
(in order of appearance)

Narrator: ....Dana Fialco

Baby Starry: ....Dana Fialco

Daddy: ....Matt Castle

Mommy: ....Dana Fialco

RoRo: ....Sharon Fialco

RayRay: ....Marvin Fialco

Rapper: ....Reggie Sinkler

Starabella: ....Dana Fialco

Come On and Be My Friend Today (Introduction) (0:15)

Music and Lyrics Written by: Tara Fialco

Piano Keyboard: Tara Fialco

Vocals: Dana Fialco

Backround Vocals: Dana Fialco

Upright Bass: Bernie Minoso

Guitar Tracks: Tony Di Lullo

Drum Programming/Percussion: Daniel Lapidus and Joe Vulpis

Additional Synthesizers/Production: Daniel Lapidus

Starabella's Lullaby (0:39)

Concept and Title by: Sharon Fialco

Music Written by: Dana Fialco

Lyrics Written by: Sharon Fialco and Dana Fialco

Piano Keyboard: Tara Fialco

Vocals: Dana Fialco

Keyboards: Daniel Lapidus

Keyboards/Synthesizers/EFX: Joe Vulpis

Bass Guitar: Joe Vulpis

Welcome to Our House (1:47)

Concept, Title, and Music Written by: Tara Fialco

Rap Written by: Sharon Fialco

Lyrics Written by: Dana Fialco

Piano: Tara Fialco

Vocals: Dana Fialco and Matt Castle

Rap: Reggie Sinkler

Background Vocals: Dana Fialco and Reggie Sinkler

Keyboards/Synthesizers/Bass: Joe Vulpis

Guitar: Tony Di Lullo

Feelings of the Past (1:05)

Concept, Title, and Music Written by: Tara Fialco

Piano Keyboard: Tara Fialco

Vocal Humming: Dana Fialco

Acoustic Guitar: Tony Di Lullo

Bass Guitar: Joe Vulpis

Keyboards/Synthesizers: Joe Vulpis

Additional Synthesizers: Daniel Lapidus

It's a Mystery (1:20)

Concept and Title by: Sharon Fialco

Music and Lyrics Written by: Joe Vulpis

Vocals: Dana Fialco and Matt Castle

Piano/Synthesizers/Bass: Joe Vulpis

Lazy Ladybug Morning (1:10)

Concept and Title by: Sharon Fialco

Music Written by: Tara Fialco

Piano: Tara Fialco

Vocal Humming: Dana Fialco

Additional Piano: Joe Vulpis

Keyboards/Synthesizers: Joe Vulpis

Determination (2:42)

Concept and Title by: Sharon Fialco

Music and Lyrics Written by: Dana Fialco

Vocals: Dana Fialco and Matt Castle

Background Vocals: Dana Fialco and Matt Castle

Keyboards/Synthesizers/B3/Bass/Programming: Joe Vulpis

Guitars: Tony Di Lullo

The Seasons Flow with Music (3:50)

Concept, Title, and Music Written by: Tara Fialco

Narration Written by: Sharon Fialco

Piano: Tara Fialco

Narration: Dana Fialco

Keyboards/Synthesizers/EFX/Orchestration/Additional Piano: Joe Vulpis

Kitten Kaboodle (1:21)

Title and Music Written by: Tara Fialco

Lyrics Written by: Tara Fialco and Dana Fialco

Vocal Arrangement Written by: Dana Fialco

Piano: Tara Fialco

Vocals: Dana Fialco

Background Vocals: Dana Fialco

Synthesizers: Daniel Lapidus

Additional Synthesizers: Joe Vulpis

All Music Copyright: © 2010 Fialco Productions, Inc.*

It's a Mystery © 2010 JV Songs

Joe Vulpis appears courtesy of AP Music, Inc.
Daniel Lapidus appears courtesy of The Pod, Audio Production, LLC
Peter Francovilla appears courtesy of Villa Musica Productions, Inc.

Recorded and Mixed at: AP Music Studios, Edgewater, NJ, Villa Musica Studios, New City, NY, and Val Hala Studios, New York, NY

Produced and Engineered by: Joe Vulpis

Additional Engineering by: Peter Francovilla and Daniel Lapidus

Mixed by: Joe Vulpis and Peter Francovilla at AP Music Studios, NY/NJ

Mastered by: Joe Vulpis and Peter Francovilla at AP Music Studios, NY/NJ, and Times Square Mastering

Musical Underscoring by: Joe Vulpis

Additional Underscoring by: Daniel Lapidus and Tara Fialco

Underscoring Consultants: Dana Fialco and Sharon Fialco

Fashion Design by Sharon Fialco:
Starry's cover ensemble; Starry's "Welcome to Our House" dress; and Starry's "Big Surprise" outfit

Our Story

BACKGROUND

My pen took off as if it were writing a story on its own. My thoughts could hardly keep up with it. Tara was now a young adult—a college graduate. What was this need to tell her story and rewind back to her earliest days? Was it the result of all the pent-up emotions I had experienced over the years, or was I channeling this from some creative source propelling me to share our experiences with younger parents and their children first starting out on their journey together—to help smooth out the terrain upon which they will travel?

ST. LOUIS, MISSOURI

Our baby girl entered the world marking the proudest moment in our lives—binding us together with a product of our love, providing us with an adorable companion to share our lives going forward. Where would our paths take us? Little did we know how much our new companion would determine that.

What a child she was! Always on the move and full of enthusiasm. Eyes bright with wonder as she explored her world. Along with great abilities and surprising musical talent, Tara would later present perplexing challenges. Was there a name for this puzzling combination? Not able to get a diagnosis, we were left with a MYSTERY.

We were set on a path that we were forced to carve for ourselves, isolated from others. We became creative in overcoming obstacles, bending and twisting to fit into the constraints of mainstream society, often finding ourselves on its periphery. Sustaining us on our journey were love, determination, and endurance. We were surrounded by beautiful music, guided by the light of HOPE.

There would be many questions without answers as Tara grew up. A diagnosis of high-functioning autism would not come until Tara was 21 years old. It unlocked some of the mysteries while opening up new ones. What was its cause? What could be done to help? These are questions faced by countless people with autistic family members today. With this diagnosis, we were no longer alone. We, together with other families, are now on a path seeking to solve this mystery, raising awareness of the prevalence of this condition, searching for a cure, and demanding social justice for our children.

HONOLULU, HAWAII

When Tara was six years old, the gift arrived that would alter our family's life. Tara's grandparents sent their piano from their home in St. Louis, Missouri, to our new home in Honolulu, Hawaii. Tara took to the piano as if it were a part of her. She memorized the sound of every key and soon taught herself to play any music she heard by ear. She began to compose her own music. Through music, she was able to express her thoughts and emotions and reflections on the world around her. The lyrics to her songs showed that she was philosophically precocious. This music would lift us up above some of the harshness in our lives to a place of joy where we experienced pride and gloried in Tara's ability and marveled at the blessing of her gift.

Tara's passage through the school system became the roughest part of our journey. She attended mainstream classes that were structured for convenience with the goals of standardization and conformity. Was it in the mind-set of society to embrace and encourage diversity? Did schools create socially sensitive environments for children with special needs? Did they accommodate unique ways of learning? Did the curricula provide the outlets that encourage growth and belief in oneself for ALL children? Were there opportunities for ALL children to make contributions to enrich their classroom communities? The answer to these questions was NO.

As a parent, I came to realize that besides the daily courage and effort it takes to deal with one's personal challenges, dealing with society can become the even bigger problem.

Often bewildered by the insensitive reaction of other children and her consequential isolation, Tara would come home to her beloved piano (the voice of her soul) and play songs of hope that reflected her belief in the potential goodness in all people. She created a musical, magical world where "all people got along and were accepted exactly the way they were." One of these songs, "Welcome to a Bright New World," became the inspiration for the Starabella series. It is in her music that Tara's generous nature lies. She shares her vision of a better world to include all people.

Dana's arrival into our family three years after Tara's brought the sunshine into our lives. Perhaps other people's days started with the rising sun, but my days did not begin until I kissed Dana good morning and she smiled her dimpled, sunny smile. I took her happy demeanor to be a reflection showing me that as far as she was concerned, I was OK. I gloried in that. Her contentment built my confidence, and we bonded quickly and easily.

Because of Dana's personality, abilities, and talent, our family's path branched off into many interesting directions. We attended school assemblies to see her honored with awards, attended chorus recitals where she was among the soloists, attended plays where she usually had the lead. By sixth grade, she had applied to and was accepted to Punahou School, a prestigious private school in Honolulu. She attended Punahou through high school. She went on to graduate from Brown University.

One person's plight in a family affects every member of that family. Dana took an early interest in Tara's circumstances and her music. Dana began writing lyrics to Tara's music, and they would later perform extensively together throughout our local community. Before one of these performances, Dana introduced Tara this way:

> "Tara has a story to tell. She tells of her experience and feelings growing up with learning differences and her struggle to understand and conform to the world around her and, ultimately, have that world enter hers to discover empathy and understanding together. Tara tells that story beautifully through inspired and inspirational music—a style all her own. She strives with her music to give people courage to reach for their dreams."

Tara's and Dana's paths intersected frequently through their music. They became connected by their musical talent and shared ideals.

We reached a joyful part of our journey when Dana and Tara made their professional debut at the ages of 11 and 14, respectively. They were hired to perform their original compositions, popular music, and Japanese songs at a shopping-center stage on weekends for the next year and a half. It was when she was performing that Tara appeared to glow with a light emanating from within. Dana was in her element, loving to perform. It was during these performances that our family was lifted to a level of joy, by the magic of music, above our daily concerns.

In 1993, Tara and Dana made their first recording of a song called "A New Beginning." Tara had composed "A New Beginning" at age 13, and Dana added the lyrics three years later when she turned 13. The song epitomizes Tara and Dana's joint musical philosophy. When they recorded the song, they hoped to remind people that it is possible and necessary not only to reach each other, but also to gain a greater sense of personal fulfillment and self-realization. They wanted to inspire their listeners to make new beginnings personally, nationally, and globally. These sentiments are just as meaningful today. Dana has recently recorded "A New Beginning" for re-release.

We would reap many rewards along our path when determination paid off. With her innate strength and determination, Tara went on to earn a certificate in Early Childhood Education from Honolulu Community College. She put her education to good use by bringing her musical message to children.

I had been Tara's study buddy. Based on what we learned about child development, I became inspired to write interactive, educational shows for children incorporating Tara's music. Together, Tara and I made props and scenery that we loaded in our station wagon along with her guitar, keyboard, and amplifier. We were "On Our Way"![1] Tara performed these shows solo, occasionally joined by Dana when she was visiting home on college breaks. Tara performed regularly in preschools, kindergarten classrooms, multiple-handicapped elementary school classrooms, day programs, after-school programs, and an intermediate special needs classroom.

[1] In reference to the instrumental "I'm on My Way."

Book Three of Starabella emerged from our observations of children at play at the schools where Tara performed. I noticed that anyone can become the object of ostracism. Combining Tara's childhood dilemmas with those of other children, the story covers a broad spectrum of social situations children confront at school every day. Some of the comments made by Starabella's classmates are the actual words of these children. In 1994, we recorded a version of the Starabella story that incorporated these observations. This version now comprises part of the current Book Three, *Starabella: Welcome to a Bright New World*.

NEW YORK, NEW YORK

Our family made its own "New Beginning" by moving to the thriving island of Manhattan. Here were occupational and artistic opportunities. Plus, there was a network of support for Tara that was unavailable in Honolulu. Tara and Dana performed extensively in many special needs venues in their first years in New York. They are now on separate career paths but still collaborate on recording projects involving their music.

Through the combined efforts of the many parents journeying on their paths, advocating for their children, there are now better educational options for children with special needs. Parents must seek out which program best serves the needs of their individual child. For parents who feel that it compromises their children's civil rights and optimal social and learning potential to be segregated into separate classrooms, more and more children are now members of inclusive classrooms.

When these programs are structured properly to meet the various needs of individual students, all children benefit. Being a member of a diverse learning environment prepares children to feel comfortable in our multicultural, diverse world. Through the Starabella stories, we hope to encourage this trend.

Children who listen to and view Books One and Two celebrate Starabella's accomplishments, feel compassion for her extra challenges, root for her to reach her goals, and gain understanding of her emotions through her music. In this way, they acquire empathy for her by the time she enters kindergarten.

In Book One, children meet Starabella and follow her through babyhood and her early toddler years in the private world of her home. She is the focus of the attention of her family, and they do all they can to meet her needs.

In Book Two, children follow Starabella as she ventures into the community, where there are demands for conformity and expectations for appropriate behaviors and following the rules. She has the supervision, support, and guidance of her parents.

In Book Three, Starabella enters the public arena of kindergarten, where children begin to make their own behavior choices and form their own rules. It is important that they have the guidance in these formative years of caring teachers like Miss Maradise to help them make rules that serve the needs of the whole. This provides firsthand experience in being responsible members of a democratic community.

Starabella and her classmates model the behavior of children who embrace diversity in their friendships and make empathetic social choices. They all work cooperatively to achieve their mutual goal of getting to a "Bright New World."

The journey of producing the Starabella books and recordings serves as a perfect example of the benefits of inclusion. Only through the diverse, creative talents and expertise of each contributor could Starabella and Company come to life.

To quote Mrs. Oclaif, "We are a lucky family," in that we had the opportunity to participate together to produce the Starabella series. Although the inspiration for writing this story stemmed from serious issues and the desire to inspire empathy in children toward one another and provide the tools for change, its actual development brought Tara, Dana, my husband Marvin, and me much joy. We hope children everywhere will see how brilliantly their eyes will shine and how they become empowered when they have the courage to act on their own to reach out a hand to another child … and see that child reach out to another child and on and on and on. These are the hands that can unite the world. "It is only up to you."[2]

[2] Lyrics from "I Can Do What I Want to Do."

Contributors

As contributors to the Starabella series, we have all come to the place where our paths meet in HARMONY.

Tara Fialco

Tara's musical compositions provided the seed from which everyone else's creativity grew. It took courage for Tara to revisit the experiences of her childhood so that other children who feel they are on the periphery of the circle of social acceptance will know they are not alone. She wants them to have the courage to keep their dreams alive and for all children to work together to create a world where everyone gets along.

Tara composed the music and wrote many of the lyrics for the musical numbers presented from Starabella's point of view—17 in all. She played the piano and keyboard for all of these songs. Many of the underscoring lines were also taken from tracks of her performances.

Dana Alexandra Fialco

Dana has been singing, performing, and writing her entire life. Her official acting debut came when she was selected to play the starring role in her first-grade play as a caterpillar who turned into a butterfly; she's had the "bug" ever since. She has most recently turned her attention to creating and performing original works.

Dana facilitated many aspects of this production. She collaborated with Joe Vulpis, our music producer, on much of the underscoring and background harmonies for the songs. She also provided me with invaluable feedback on the scripts.

Dana's talents are multifaceted, and her performance on the Starabella CDs sparkles. As the stories' narrator, she created distinctly unique personalities and voices for 13 characters. She composed and wrote the music and lyrics for four original songs, one performed by the teacher and three performed by the parents. The tenderness of her performance reflects her empathy for the characters.

Sharon Fialco

I directed this project, wrote the scripts, and together with my husband, Marvin, published the Starabella series. Marvin and I have been privileged to have our lives filled with the beautiful music of our two wonderful daughters. Much of our family's journey is reflected in this music. I enjoyed providing the words that tied these musical stories together. I also had the opportunity to try my hand at some lyric writing. As an extra bonus, I had fun applying my hobby as a clothes designer to create much of the wardrobe for the stories' characters.

Producing this project has enhanced my life with special meaning and purpose.

J. Marvin Fialco

Marvin is a graduate of the Harvard Business School and Brown University. He was president of Hawaiian King Candies in Honolulu, HI, for 30 years. Marvin's belief in us and in the value of this project for individuals and society as a whole provided Tara, Dana, and me the confidence to persevere in turning our family's dream into reality. He counseled us and we relied on his feedback every step of the way. Without his practical and emotional support, this project would not have been possible.

Gia Williams

Gia is an actress, cabaret artist, and TV hostess. She has toured nationally with the Harlem Gospel Choir and internationally with the Harlem Gospel Ensemble. Her warmth and friendly enthusiasm shine through her stellar performance of Miss Maradise, Starabella's kindergarten teacher.

Matt Castle

Matt Castle is a versatile actor and musician who has appeared in plays, operas, and musical productions across the United States. In 2006, he made his Broadway debut playing Peter in the